# BEAR ON A BIKE

**Written by Stella Blackstone**
**Illustrated by Debbie Harter**

**Barefoot Books**
Step inside a story

Bear on a bike,
As happy as can be,
Where are you going, Bear?
Please wait for me!

I'm going to the market,
Where fruit and flowers are sold,
Where people buy fresh oranges
And pots of marigold.

Bear on a raft,
As happy as can be,
Where are you going, Bear?
Please wait for me!

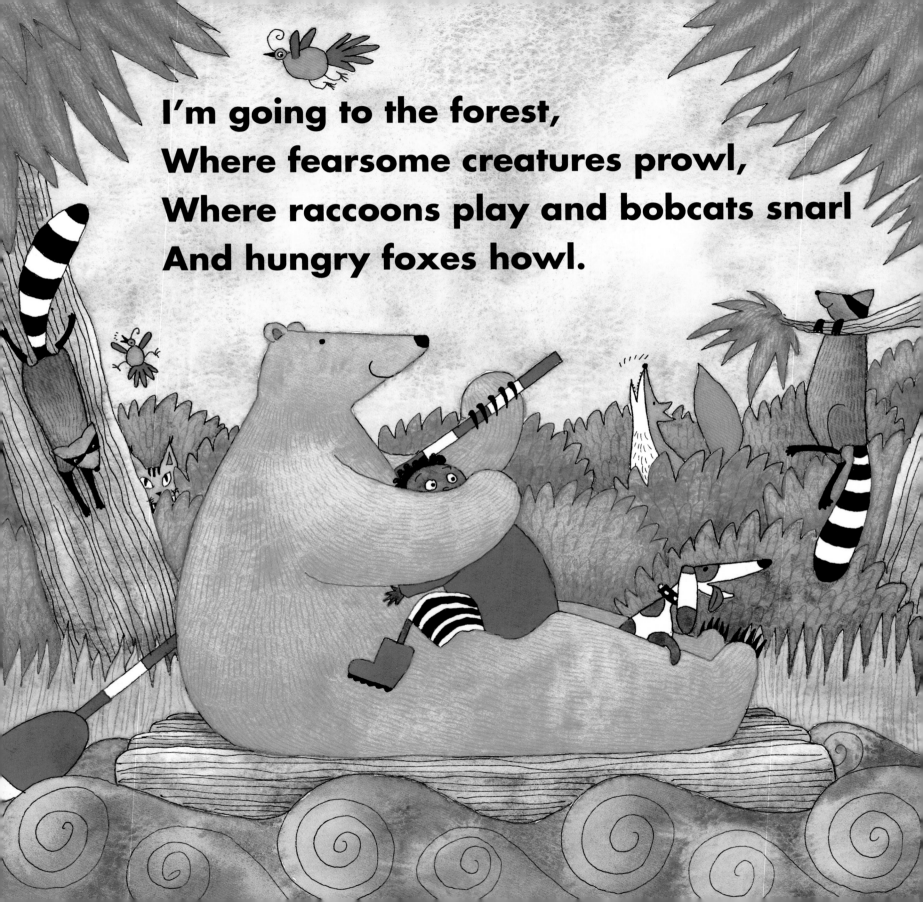

I'm going to the forest,
Where fearsome creatures prowl,
Where raccoons play and bobcats snarl
And hungry foxes howl.

Bear on a wagon,
As happy as can be,
Where are you going, Bear?
Please wait for me!

I'm going to the prairie,
Where wild buffaloes roam,
Where graceful eagles soar and glide
And prairie dogs make their home.

Bear in a steam train,
As happy as can be,
Where are you going, Bear?
Please wait for me!

I'm going to the seaside,
Where children love to play,
Where young friends dig and race
And swim, while fishes dart away.

Bear on a boat,
As happy as can be,
Where are you going, Bear?
Please wait for me!

I'm going to an island,
Where magic star fruits grow,
Where herons fish in secret groves
And sparkling rivers flow.

Bear in a balloon,
As happy as can be,
Where are you going, Bear?
Please wait for me!

I'm going to a rainbow,
Where the earth meets the sky,
Where the clouds turn into rain
And bright-winged parrots fly.

Bear in a carriage,
As happy as can be,
Where are you going, Bear?
Please wait for me!

I'm going to a castle,
Where night is turned to day,
Where princes and princesses dance
And merry music plays.

Bear on a rocket,
Flying through the night,
Wherever you are going, Bear,
Goodbye and goodnight!

# For more fun with Bear:

Text copyright © 1998 by Stella Blackstone
Illustrations copyright © 1998 by Debbie Harter
The moral rights of Stella Blackstone and Debbie Harter have been asserted

First published in Great Britain by Barefoot Books, Ltd
and in the United States of America by Barefoot Books, Inc in 1998
The paperback edition first published in 2006
The boardbook edition first published in 2001
All rights reserved

Graphic design by Jennie Hoare, Bradford-on-Avon, UK
Reproduction by Unifoto, Cape Town
Printed in China on 100% acid-free paper

This book was typeset in Slappy and Futura
The illustrations were prepared in paint,
pen and ink, and crayon

Paperback ISBN 978-1-90523-698-5
Boardbook ISBN 978-1-84148-374-0

British Cataloguing-in-Publication Data:
a catalogue record for this book is available from the British Library
Library of Congress Cataloging-in-Publication Data
is available upon request

Barefoot Books, 294 Banbury Road, Oxford, OX2 7ED
Barefoot Books, 2067 Massachusetts Ave, Cambridge, MA 02140

21